A Journey Through Triumph and Tragedy

I0533613

By
Milky Harris

Copyright © 2025 by Milky Harris

All rights reserved. No part of this book may be reproduced, distributed, or transmitted in any form or by any means, including photocopying, recording, or other electronic or mechanical methods, without the prior written permission of the publisher, except in the case of brief quotations embodied in critical reviews and certain other non-commercial uses permitted by copyright law.

DEDICATION

This book is dedicated to my deceased daughter.

ACKNOWLEDGMENT

This book would not have been possible without the love, support, and encouragement of so many people along the way.

To my **family**—thank you for being my foundation, my greatest source of love, and my reason for pushing forward through every challenge.

To my **friends and loved ones**—thank you for sharing in my journey, for the laughter, the memories, and the lessons we have learned together.

To those who have been part of my travels—whether for a fleeting moment or a lasting friendship—thank you for showing me the beauty of human connection.

To **Isabella, Sabrina, and the entire team** who helped bring this book to life—thank you for believing in my story and helping me share it with the world.

And finally, to **you, the reader**—thank you for taking this journey with me. May you find inspiration, hope, and a renewed sense of adventure in your own life.

The world is waiting.

Go explore it.

ABOUT THE AUTHOR

Milky Harris was born on March 31st, 1956, in Rochford, Essex. He attended Long Road Junior School and Furtherwick Park Senior School, leaving at 16. Though he had no formal higher education, he excelled in arts and sports, particularly rugby, football, and long-distance running.

After school, Milky held various jobs, including work in a builder's yard, suspended ceilings, and a position at *Ford Motor Company* until a back injury in 1983 led to early retirement. Despite facing personal and health challenges in the years that followed, he found moments of work in air-conditioning and landscaping.

A lifelong lover of art, music, and film, Milky continues to pursue his passions in retirement. He enjoys painting, traveling, dancing to Motown and soul, and watching classic cinema. Active and social, he spends his time walking, jogging, playing snooker, indoor bowls, chess, and golf. He now resides in a uniquely styled log-cabin cottage that reflects his creative spirit and individuality.

These days, Milky also does inspirational speeches for people in need, so he can spread hope and love to them all and inspire them to grow into the best versions of themselves.

TABLE OF CONTENT

INTRODUCTION

This is not just an essay about the life experiences that I have had throughout my life; it is a tapestry woven from the threads of emotion, resilience, and transformation. This book is an entire emotion, a journey through triumph and tragedy, written to convey a powerful message by a layman, born and bred in Canvey lands. This book is a little effort of the ordinary man to bring change to the lives of the people by giving them the message of optimism. This book is purposefully written to inspire those who feel lost in the darkness, overwhelmed by dissatisfaction, and on the brink of giving up. It's a deep analysis of the sorts that have shaped me, a record of my life's journey through thick and thin.

Life, as I have lived it, has been far from idyllic. It has been marked by daunting challenges, unimaginable tragedies, and moments of excruciating pain. There were times when I found myself navigating paths I never imagined I would have to walk. Yet, beneath these adversities lay hidden messages, waiting patiently to be uncovered. Each setback carried within it a lesson, a whisper of wisdom guiding me through tumultuous times. These difficulties were not merely obstacles; they were veils that shrouded insights capable of illuminating my way forward.

I was fortunate to step into the spotlight as the Milky Bar Kid, a role that brought with it a unique blend of joy and challenges. Though financial constraints eventually ended my time in that world, it was a pivotal moment in my life. It was more than just a role—it was an awakening. That chapter helped me clear the fog clouding my vision and allowed me to explore what had been hidden inside me. Becoming the Milky Bar Kid became a turning point that shaped the course of my journey, teaching me lessons far beyond the surface of childhood fame.

In these pages, I would like my readers not just to learn how I walk through life's challenges but also to be a significant lesson for them. As you read through this book, you'll come to understand that life is synonymous with endless challenges and growth. Each moment brings new experiences, lessons, and opportunities to evolve. Life is a journey filled with joy, sorrow, success, and failure, continually testing our strength and resilience as we search for purpose and meaning. Through my experiences, I hope to inspire you to embrace life's trials and find strength in every obstacle you face.

At some point in life, you break down and lose your direction due to overwhelming challenges, and you feel suffocated by the weight of it all. But this is precisely the moment where your resilience is truly tested. It's in these dark times that the strength of your spirit shines through. The beauty of life lies not in avoiding challenges but in embracing them and discovering the happiness and growth that emerge from the struggle. Life is never a straight path; it is full of ups and downs, and those who navigate its turbulence with grace and determination are the ones who thrive. The strongest individuals are those who understand that setbacks are not the end but an opportunity for a fresh start. Only those who live fully recognize that there may come a time when you feel abandoned or betrayed by life's deceptions, but even in those moments, there is always a way forward. It's the willingness to rise from adversity that ultimately defines the quality of one's life.

PART – I

BEGINNINGS ON CANVEY ISLAND

CHAPTER 1

A BEAUTIFUL ISLAND CHILDHOOD

Canvey Island was my cradle, my playground, and the backdrop of my earliest memories. Born on March 31, 1956, I grew up nestled in the embrace of this lovely island, surrounded by the shimmering waters of the Thames Estuary. To me, it was more than just a piece of land; it was a world bursting with beauty and wonder. I remember the sea views, stretching endlessly, and the lush green forests that bordered one side of our little community. In those days, open spaces were abundant, and they became the canvas for my childhood adventures.

My childhood was a patchwork of vibrant moments shared with my family. My parents, strong and nurturing, shaped my early years in ways I would only come to appreciate later. My father was a Docker, a hardworking man who spent his days at the docks and his evenings managing a semi-professional football team. He was a stern figure, but in his strength, I found comfort. My mother, on the other hand, was the heart of our family. Everyone adored her—her warmth and kindness drew people in, and I was no exception. She was my rock, the one who guided me through my days, taking me to school and cheering me on in everything I did.

Life on Canvey Island was filled with the joys of childhood. I spent countless hours playing football in the fields, mushrooming in the woods, with friends. We were a band of mischievous children, exploring every nook and cranny, collecting bird's eggs (even if it was a bit naughty), and forging bonds that would last a lifetime. I can still feel the thrill of those sunny afternoons, the laughter echoing around us as we played games until the sun dipped below the horizon.

But life wasn't always idyllic. My early years were marked by hardships that tested my spirit. At the tender age of three, I underwent surgery for a squint. I was whisked away to South End Hospital, where I spent six long weeks. In the sterile world of the hospital, I found solace in the company of an elderly gentleman. I would crawl into his bed, seeking comfort in his presence as I lay there, my young mind

4

struggling to comprehend the gravity of my situation. My parents were always nearby, their concern palpable, but it was this gentle soul who offered me warmth when I needed it most.

Just a couple of years later, my innocence was further shattered when I was struck by a car at five. The memory is hazy, but I recall the pain and confusion, the eight weeks spent in the hospital as I healed from my injuries. They told my parents I was lucky to be alive. Those experiences, both traumatic and formative, taught me resilience, though at the time, I didn't fully grasp their impact.

As I navigated the ups and downs of my childhood, I found a peculiar sort of fame. People often remarked on how much I resembled the Milky Bar Kid, a character from a popular TV advert. Back then, with only three channels to choose from—BBC One, BBC Two, and ITV—advertisements felt monumental. In 1963, I was whisked away for an audition that would change my life, if only for a fleeting moment. My parents, supportive and excited, brought me to the city, where I found myself among other hopeful kids. When I got the nod, I stepped into a world of lights and cameras, where I would become the second Milky Bar Kid. It was an adventure that introduced me to new people, new experiences, and the thrill of being in the spotlight.

School life rolled on with its usual rhythm. My primary school was a stone's throw from our home, and my days were filled with laughter and learning. I was just an average student, but the title of "Milky Bar Kid" followed me, bringing a mix of admiration and envy from my peers. As time passed, I embraced this identity, and "Milky" became a name that echoed through the years.

Through it all, my relationship with my younger brother, Tracy, was unique. He was a couple of years my junior, and while we loved each other, our interests diverged. I was drawn to older friends, those who guided me and introduced me to new adventures. Our paths didn't often cross, but I cherished the bond we shared, a subtle connection that was ours alone.

Looking back, Canvey Island wasn't just where I grew up; it was a tapestry woven with love, pain, adventure, and resilience. Those early years shaped me, laying the foundation for the man I would become, and despite the challenges, they were, in many ways, the most beautiful years of my life.

As the sun dipped below the horizon, painting the sky in hues of orange and pink, I would often sit with my family, recounting the adventures of the day. My brother, Tracy, would lean in, eyes wide with curiosity, hanging onto every word. Our little home was filled with laughter and warmth, a sanctuary from the outside world, where the challenges of life faded into the background.

My parents were the cornerstone of our family. My mother, with her boundless love and unwavering support, was the gentle heart that held us together. I can still picture her in the kitchen, the scent of freshly baked bread wafting through the air as she hummed softly to herself. She was our anchor, the one who encouraged my artistic dreams, telling me that my talent was a gift meant to be shared. Her belief in me was unwavering, and it was through her that I learned the importance of kindness and empathy.

Then there was my father, a man of strength and integrity, who worked tirelessly to provide for our family. His hands were calloused from years of labor at the docks, but it was in those moments of quiet reflection, after a long day, that I saw the love in his eyes. He had a no-nonsense approach to life, instilling in me the values of hard work and determination. I admired his ability to command respect on the football pitch, not just as a player but as a manager, where he mentored young men who looked up to him. Those experiences, watching him lead with authority, taught me lessons in responsibility and discipline that would shape my character in the years to come.

Tracy and I shared a bond that, though quiet, was ever-present. We had our own unique paths, and while we didn't always play together, we understood each other in ways that only siblings could. He often sought the solace of our home, where the chaos of the outside world faded into silence. I admired his curiosity and creativity, and even though we had different interests, I felt a sense of responsibility toward him. I wanted to be a good role model, to guide him through the challenges that lay ahead, just as our parents had guided us.

The island itself was a tapestry of beauty, woven together with the threads of community and nature. I spent hours exploring the fields, where wildflowers danced in the gentle breeze, and the sound of laughter echoed in the distance. The trees became our fortresses, and the sandy shores, our playground. We would run barefoot, the cool earth beneath our feet grounding us in the moment, as we climbed trees and chased after the setting sun. Those golden days were a kaleidoscope of color, filled with the sweet taste of freedom and the intoxicating scent of adventure.

On weekends, we'd venture to the beach, where the waves would crash against the shore, and I would dig my toes into the wet sand. The salty air wrapped around me like a familiar embrace, while I watched the boats glide across the water. I often dreamed of sailing away, of discovering distant lands where the horizon met the sea. It was a child's fantasy, yet the allure of those dreams fueled my imagination, whispering promises of what lay beyond the horizon.

But even in this idyllic setting, shadows occasionally crept into our lives. My early surgeries lingered in the back of my mind, the memories of hospital stays and the comforting presence of the elderly gentleman during my eye operation. Those moments taught me resilience, a lesson I carried into my adolescence. I learned that pain could coexist with beauty and that every scar told a story worth telling.

Then, there was the accident. The memory of being struck by a car at five still sends shivers down my spine. I was a small boy, fragile and delicate, but the strength of my spirit shone through even in the face of adversity. My parents were my lifeline during those turbulent weeks in the hospital. Their love and unwavering support helped me navigate the physical and emotional scars I carried, reminding me that I was not alone in my journey.

Reflecting on those formative years, I realize that every experience, every laugh and tear, contributed to the tapestry of who I was becoming. Canvey Island was more than just a backdrop; it was a character in my story—a place that shaped my identity and instilled within me a profound appreciation for the beauty in life's complexities.

As I continued to grow, I discovered a world filled with possibilities, interwoven with moments of joy and sorrow. The island, with its gentle landscapes and vibrant community, became a foundation upon which I would build my dreams. My childhood was a kaleidoscope of experiences, each color adding depth and richness to my story. And in the heart of it all, I found the love of my family, a guiding light that would carry me through the challenges ahead.

I often reflect on those simpler times with a sense of nostalgia, cherishing the innocence of my youth while embracing the lessons learned along the way. Canvey Island will forever be a part of me, its beauty etched in my heart, guiding me as I navigate the uncharted waters of life, reminding me that, no matter where I go, I carry with me the essence of my beginnings.

CHAPTER 2

EARLY TRAUMAS

Life, a delicate and relentless dance, has a way of weaving meaning into our existence—sometimes in soft, nurturing patterns, and other times with the harsh strokes of tragedy. Each experience, though painful, becomes a stepping stone, shaping us and, perhaps, even arming us with strength and resilience. Yet trauma leaves its indelible mark, not just on our hearts but on our minds, reshaping us, for better or worse, into who we are destined to be.

I was only three years old when I faced my first major battle. Life should have been simple then, full of endless play and innocent wonder. Instead, I found myself in South End Hospital, my tiny body bracing for eye surgery. The world around me felt cold and clinical, the air heavy with the sharp scent of antiseptic. It was a space far removed from the safety of home, and I had no words to describe the fear that gripped me.

The days turned into weeks—six long weeks of hospital lights and echoing footsteps. I remember the haze of doctors and nurses, the masks hiding any comforting expressions. There were moments when fear consumed me, but then, amid the sterile walls, I discovered a source of comfort in the form of an elderly gentleman. We shared the same ward, and though I was just a child, he became my quiet refuge.

He welcomed me without question, a gentle smile always lighting his face. Sometimes, when the fear of the unknown became too overwhelming, I would crawl into his bed, seeking the warmth that only human connection could provide. There, the nights felt less lonely, the looming shadows softened by the presence of this unexpected friend. For six weeks, he was my sanctuary, a source of light in the darkness that surgery had cast on my young world.

When the hospital finally released me, I emerged with glasses and a new understanding of fragility. My parents, always trying to be strong, never spoke of how much those weeks had taken from them, but I could feel their silent pain. It was a chapter closed, yet the trauma of those days lingered, a quiet whisper that would follow me through life.

Life, unpredictable as ever, struck again two years later. I was five, just a boy exploring the world with wide-eyed curiosity. I don't remember why I was out that day, but I'll never forget what came next. The car appeared like a flash of lightning, and in a terrifying instant, my young body was flung like a rag doll, a mere toy against the brute force of metal and speed.

I don't recall the exact moment of impact, but the aftermath is a blur of pain and terror. My body was broken in ways a five-year-old should never endure. Bones shattered, and I lay on the brink of death. My parents were told how close I was to slipping away, a piece of information that seared itself into their hearts. The hospital became my world once again, and this time, I was there for eight excruciating weeks.

I fought to recover, my small form enduring more than it should have ever had to. My mother's eyes were pools of worry, and my father's tough exterior seemed to harden even more, masking the anguish he didn't know how to share. Trauma doesn't just impact the one who suffers; it sends shockwaves through an entire family, bending but not breaking the bonds that hold loved ones together.

The car accident left more than physical scars. It left a legacy of pain and strength, a paradox that would shape my life in ways I couldn't yet understand. As I healed, my spirit, though shaken, began to mend alongside my body. I was learning, even then, that life doesn't come with the promise of fairness. Yet it seemed to whisper that there was a reason behind every challenge, even if the reasons remained shrouded in mystery.

Trauma, I would come to learn, never truly fades. It lingers as a constant companion that reshapes your very being. For some, it triggers hyper-independence, a fierce determination never to be vulnerable again. For others, it becomes a silent shadow, influencing decisions and relationships in imperceptible ways. But through it all, there is strength in survival, a stubborn light that refuses to go out.

Recovery from the accident was slow and grueling, but eventually, life found a way to return to a semblance of normalcy. I was still so young, yet the weight of those early traumas had aged me in ways that weren't visible. My body had healed, but my mind was forever altered. Each step I took, each game I played, carried with it the whisper of what had been—a fear that something else might be lurking just around the corner.

My parents did what they could to shield me from the world's harshness, though I could see the worry etched in their eyes, the way they hovered a little closer and gripped my hand a little tighter. My mother, always a loving presence, tried to bring back the simple joys of childhood. She was my anchor, the one who made me feel safe when everything else seemed uncertain. Her gentle touch and her whispered reassurances, became my lifelines. My father, on the other hand, embodied strength. He worked tirelessly at the docks, and though he wasn't home much, his presence was a reminder of resilience.

I knew that they loved me fiercely, but love doesn't always have the power to erase trauma. My young heart had felt the sting of fear, and my mind had begun to build walls, each brick a response to the pain. These were the early seeds of what I would come to understand as a trauma response—an instinctive, protective armor I wore even as I tried to rediscover my place in the world.

Despite the hardships, there were moments of light. I tried to hold on to the small joys, the games in the fields, and the laughter that spilled out when my friends and I played make-believe adventures. Yet, I was no longer the carefree child I had once been. The surgery and the accident had changed me, even if I couldn't fully grasp how. I craved control over my world, a fierce independence that seemed to grow stronger with each passing day.

It was as if a part of me had decided that I could never again afford to feel helpless. This newfound hyper-independence was both a shield and a burden. I wanted to be strong, to prove to the world—and perhaps to myself—that I could endure anything. But deep down, I was still that little boy who had found solace in the warmth of an elderly man's embrace, still that fragile child who had faced death and survived.

The world kept moving, even as I tried to piece myself back together. There were birthday celebrations and new friendships, bike rides along the dusty roads of our small community, and lazy afternoons picking blackberries. But alongside the innocence of childhood was a thread of fear, a constant reminder that life could be ripped away at any moment. It wasn't something I could articulate back then; it was simply a feeling, a knowledge I carried quietly.

Looking back, I understand now that those early experiences left deep imprints. They set the stage for how I would face future trials, how I would learn to navigate a world that, at times, felt cruel and unpredictable. The scars, both physical and emotional, became part of my story. Yet, despite the darkness, there was always a flicker of hope—a stubborn belief that life, for all its pain, still held meaning, still had a purpose.

And so, I continued on, a child touched by trauma but determined to carve out a life worth living. Each step forward was a defiance of what had tried to break me, and each breath was a promise that I would keep going, no matter what.

CHAPTER 3

BECOMING THE MILKY BAR KID

Life is full of unexpected turns, moments that define us in ways we never could have imagined. For me, one of those moments came when I was just a boy on Canvey Island, blissfully unaware that a simple resemblance would change my life forever. It all began at a family wedding, a day that seemed ordinary until it wasn't.

I never could have predicted that my life would intersect with a famous television icon, but that day, everything shifted. People had always commented on how much I looked like the Milky Bar Kid, with my blonde hair, glasses, and the innocent mischief that lit up my face. But at that wedding, fate intervened in a way I couldn't understand then. The sister of the original Milky Bar Kid happened to be there, and she noticed the striking resemblance. She must have felt a sense of urgency, a need to tell someone who could make something happen. Before long, the people in charge of the Milky Bar Kid ads contacted my parents, asking if I'd come to London for an audition.

I was only six or seven, and I remember the excitement buzzing through our house. My parents were proud but cautious, and I felt the thrill that comes with new possibilities. London was a world away from our quiet life on Canvey Island, and when my parents took me there, the experience was surreal. At the audition, I found myself surrounded by 12 to 15 other hopeful kids, all dressed up in the iconic cowboy hat, glasses, and suit. It felt like a game, yet one with stakes I couldn't quite comprehend. We rehearsed lines and acted out scenes, and while I was just a boy having fun, I sensed that my resemblance to the original Milky Bar Kid set me apart. By the end of the day, I got the nod—I was going to be the new Milky Bar Kid.

The role itself was a whirlwind adventure, full of excitement and challenges. For a young lad from Canvey Island, the glitz of London was both enchanting and intimidating. I would travel up to the city, but unlike many child stars today, my parents couldn't always accompany me. They were working-class people, tied to their responsibilities back home, and so arrangements were made for me to stay with others. I can't recall now if these people were relatives or friends, but I do remember feeling very far from home.

Filming was thrilling yet unsettling. There I was, a young boy, thrust into a bustling world of cameras, directors, and bright lights. While I tried to soak it all in, part of me longed for the comfort of Canvey Island, where life was simple and familiar. I missed playing in the fields, the sand between my toes, and the sea views that always felt like home. It was a strange paradox: I was living a dream, one many kids might have envied, but I couldn't shake the homesickness that clung to me. Each time the cameras stopped rolling, I would count down the days until I could return to my world, to my family, and to the laughter of friends who knew me as Milky, not just the Milky Bar Kid.

Despite the discomfort, there were moments of genuine joy. Wearing that cowboy outfit made me feel special like I had a secret identity. I would recite the famous lines, bringing the character to life, and it was exhilarating to know that kids all over the country would see me on TV. Yet behind the excitement, there was a lingering sense of vulnerability, of being a small boy playing a very big part.

The role didn't last forever, and looking back, the reasons were understandable, even if they were tinged with disappointment. My family's financial and logistical struggles were hard to overcome. My parents didn't have a car, and traveling to London from Canvey Island was an ordeal, involving buses, trains, and a level of effort we couldn't always afford. My father worked tirelessly at the docks, while my mother was caring for me and my younger brother, Trace.

Pursuing a career in show business requires a relentless commitment, and my parents, as much as they loved me, couldn't keep up with the demands. They were hardworking people, doing their best with what they had. In the end, the world of acting slipped away. The Milky Bar Kid was just a chapter, one that couldn't be sustained. I often wondered if things might have been different had we lived closer to London or had more resources. But as a young boy, I was mostly relieved to return to Canvey Island, to my familiar world and simple joys.

What surprised me, though, was the legacy the role left behind. I didn't realize at the time how much it would shape me, even beyond childhood. Being the Milky Bar Kid became part of my identity, something that people in my community celebrated. The nickname "Milky" stuck, and it became something I cherished. It defined me, in a way, and gave me a story that I would carry into adulthood with pride. It wasn't just about fame; it was about belonging, about being remembered for something unique.

Even now, all these years later, I hold on to that identity. I've often joked that when my time comes, I want my name on my gravestone to be "Milky Harris." It's a playful but deeply meaningful tribute to a role that, while brief, gave me a lifetime of memories and a name that still makes people smile.

Being the Milky Bar Kid taught me more than lines or how to stand in front of a camera. It taught me about resilience, about navigating life's highs and lows, and about the simple power of a legacy, no matter how small. I learned that sometimes the most important things are what we carry forward, the stories that connect us to our past and shape who we become. And for me, it all started with a boy who looked like the Milky Bar Kid, a cowboy hat, and a dream that lived just long enough to leave a lasting mark.

The Gift That Keeps Giving

Even now, so many years later, being the Milky Bar Kid feels like a gift that keeps on giving. It's a story that never fails to draw smiles, whether I'm meeting someone new or catching up with old friends. The memories of that time, though distant, are preserved in the way people respond when they hear my name. I still get a rush of warmth when someone calls out, "Milky!" It's a reminder that, in some small way, I've left a mark.

The funny thing is, the identity I took on as the Milky Bar Kid became a source of unexpected strength. It taught me about the power of being remembered, about how even fleeting experiences can shape us forever. It gave me a sense of belonging, an acknowledgment that, for a brief moment, I was part of something bigger than myself. And in a world where so many of us search for a place to belong, that feeling is a rare and precious treasure.

I've often reflected on how that time molded me. The resilience I developed from being away from home, the way I learned to navigate unfamiliar environments, and the quiet pride I carried back to Canvey Island—it all stayed with me. Those experiences didn't just give me a nickname; they formed a part of my character, adding depth to my understanding of myself and my place in the world. Even the discomfort and homesickness became lessons, teaching me about the value of family and the pull of home.

The world has changed so much since those days. When I was the Milky Bar Kid, there were only three television stations and an advert like ours was a big deal, seen by nearly everyone. Today, there are hundreds of channels and endless ways to consume content, making it hard to imagine just how significant those ads were back then. It was a simpler time, a world where fame was something entirely different— more innocent, perhaps, or at least more localized.

But the essence of the Milky Bar Kid has persisted. Children still recognize the iconic character, and adults fondly remember the ads from their youth. Being part of something that continues to bring joy and nostalgia is a privilege I never take for granted. It's as though I am part of a legend, a small but cherished piece of collective memory.

When I look at the memorabilia—old photos, advertisements, and the cowboy hat I once wore—it all feels surreal. But the memories remain vivid, filled with the laughter and excitement of a boy who was lucky enough to live a dream, even if only for a while. I've shared those stories with my family, and they've become a part of our history, too. My daughter and grandson love hearing the tales, and I find joy in passing them down, and in keeping the magic alive.

One of the most meaningful parts of being the Milky Bar Kid is how it has shaped not only my identity but also my hopes for future generations. I want my family to feel the same pride in their roots, and to understand that even the smallest moments can define who we are. It's why I've told my daughter that, when the time comes, I want to be remembered as Milky Harris. I want that name to live on, a testament to a life that was, in many ways, extraordinary.

There's a lightness to being Milky, a playful side of me that has never quite disappeared. Perhaps it's because I've carried a piece of that carefree, adventurous boy with me into adulthood. Even as life presented its challenges, that part of me stayed hopeful, always seeing the humor and joy in things. It's a gift I hope to share with everyone I meet, a reminder that even brief moments of fame or recognition can leave an enduring legacy.

Being the Milky Bar Kid wasn't just a role I played; it became a part of my spirit. And as I continue to move through life, I hold onto that spirit with pride and gratitude. It's more than a fond memory—it's a symbol of resilience, of family, and of the unexpected ways life can surprise us. Because, in the end, the story of the Milky Bar Kid isn't just about the ads or the character; it's about how a little boy from Canvey Island found a way to leave his mark on the world.

PART – II
FAMILY AND EARLY LIFE

CHAPTER 4

GROWING UP

Childhood was a world of contrasts, shaped by the unique energies of my parents. My mother was the epitome of warmth and compassion, a woman with a rare gift for making everyone feel at ease. She had this magnetic charm, a way of drawing people in and leaving them lighter, happier, just for having been near her. Friends from the neighborhoods loved coming over, not just for the games or the occasional biscuits she'd hand out but simply for her presence. She was the heart of our home, creating an environment where I always felt seen and cared for.

My father, on the other hand, was a man of strength and precision, someone who commanded respect in every aspect of his life. He worked long hours at the docks, often gone before I was awake and returning home only after the sun had set. But his real passion was football. When I was old enough—around eight or nine—I started accompanying him to the matches he coached. That's where I saw another side of him, a side that fascinated me. On the pitch, he was a force, someone who could organize, motivate, and inspire grown men. He didn't need to raise his voice often; there was something in the way he carried himself that naturally drew attention.

Watching him from the sidelines, I felt a surge of pride and awe. It wasn't just his skill in managing a team that impressed me—it was the respect he commanded and the authority he carried effortlessly. I loved being in that environment, surrounded by the energy of the players, the shouts and whistles, and the clatter of boots against the grass. It became a shared space for us, a bond that grew stronger with every match I watched by his side.

At home, life found a rhythm between the quiet love of my mother and the structured influence of my father. My days were filled with school, sports, and the occasional escapade with friends. School was never about academics for me; it was the sports field where I felt most alive. Rugby and football became an extension of my father's world, a way for me to carve out my own identity while still feeling connected to him. Influenced by my father, I also played football in the local leagues. Though I'd admit that I wasn't as skillful as many of the other players on the field, I was good enough to be known as the Milky Kid by the people from different clubs and opposing teams. I loved the rush of feelings it gave me, as if, I was carrying with me what my father had built and established over the years.

My father, who managed semi-professional teams, had a significant influence on my early football experiences. When I was around 19 or 20, he invited me and a few players from my local team to play a friendly game against his team, which had much better players. This was a big deal for us. I was eager to prove myself against these superior players.

I played for only about 5 or 10 minutes, during which I went into several tackles. I was really getting into it! Suddenly, my father stopped the game and took me off. I was gutted. When I asked him why, he said, 'Son, my players have an important game this weekend, and if I left you on, you would have injured some of them. You were like a raging bull!'

At the time, I was disappointed, but later, my father and I laughed about it. It became a funny memory of my early football days.

The Milky Bar Kid role added another layer to my childhood. It set me apart in a way that was both thrilling and challenging. Everyone in the neighborhood knew me; I was "the kid from the adverts." It brought a sense of pride but also an awareness that I was carrying something unique. My classmates often looked at me with a mix of fascination and envy, and while I enjoyed the attention, it sometimes made me feel like I was living under a spotlight.

Through it all, my mother remained my unwavering source of support. She seemed to understand the pressures of that early fame without me ever having to say a word. When I came home after a long day at school or from a particularly rough rugby practice, she was always there with a smile, a kind word, or my favorite meal waiting on the table. Her love was the constant in my life, a reminder that no matter how much the world outside demanded of me, I would always have a place to return to.

My father's influence was different but equally profound. He taught me the value of discipline, of showing up and giving your best no matter the circumstances. Watching him manage his football teams, I learned about leadership—not just the kind that commands respect but the kind that inspires loyalty. It wasn't until much later in life that I realized how much of him I carried in me, how his strength and determination had quietly shaped the person I was becoming.

While growing up, another character who had a very strong influence on me was my football team manager. His name was Roy McDonald, but we all knew him as "Mac." My team was called Mornington Boys F.C., and Mac ran the whole club. He was a great guy and was always very supportive of me and all the boys.

As mentioned before, I had this "very tough tackler on the football pitch" image about me, and Mac would always encourage me—yet he also taught me to control and discipline my aggression, most of the time. (It didn't always work!) But throughout my teenage years, I had great respect for him.

As I got older, life took us on different paths and we lost contact for a number of years. But many years later, I got back in touch with Mac, and we reminisced and smiled about those early days of growing up. He has since passed, but I remember him with great fondness.

Another little story from that time... As I said, I had that hardman image on the pitch and was well-known for it in the local football leagues—and admittedly, I loved it.

At an end-of-season football presentation night, all the teams from our league were present. My team then was Delta Sports F.C., and that year we had won both the league and the cup. After we had received our medals, along with other teams, the presenter took the microphone and addressed the crowd:

"Please everyone, we have one final presentation to make. We'd like to present these illegal metal studs—along with a new pair of football laces—to Milky Harris, the hardman of the league. His old studs and laces must be worn out and clogged with blood from all the tackles he's done!"

I got some whoops and muted cheers for that one—I'm not sure all of them were approved, but I loved it. Among the several trophies and medals I've collected over the years, that one—Hardman of the League, 1975—along with my 1990 London Marathon medal, are two of my most prized.

Looking back, those years were a delicate dance between two worlds— one of unconditional love and another of ambition and resilience. Together, they laid the foundation for the person I would grow into, grounding me in the lessons of family, hard work, and the enduring power of connection.

CHAPTER 5

SIBLING DYNAMICS

Tracy—now Trace—was my younger brother by two and a half years, though the gap often felt wider as we grew up. As kids, our relationship was a mixture of familial affection and inevitable distance. I loved him, of course, but we were very different people, even from a young age. While I gravitated toward older kids and sought adventure, Tracy was content in his own world, mixing with friends closer to his age.

I was always on the move, pushing boundaries, drawn to sports and the whirlwind of activity that came with being "the Milky Bar Kid." That title set me apart, and I embraced it with pride. Tracy, on the other hand, lived outside of that sphere, carving out his own quieter path. We existed in the same household, but in many ways, we were on parallel tracks, rarely intersecting.

As we moved into our teenage years, the differences between us became even more pronounced. I was drawn to rugby and football, chasing the rugged camaraderie and discipline of team sports. Tracy, however, found his passion in bodybuilding. It suited his personality— focused, solitary, and deliberate. Where I thrived in the chaos of competition, he found solace in the quiet intensity of lifting weights.

Despite our diverging interests, I admired his dedication. He poured himself into bodybuilding with the same focus I gave to my sports, transforming his physique and building a sense of identity through the discipline it demanded. Still, our paths rarely crossed in any meaningful way. We were brothers, but we weren't close in the way you might expect siblings to be.

When we both reached adulthood, life carried us in completely different directions. Tracy eventually moved to Ibiza, embracing a lifestyle that couldn't have been further removed from mine. He became deeply spiritual, immersing himself in a way of life I struggled to understand. It wasn't my world, and it certainly wasn't a world we could share.

23

Our father's illness in 2017 marked a turning point in our relationship, though not for the better. Tracy, still living abroad, had his own views about how Dad's care should be handled. Those months were tense, filled with long-distance disagreements and unspoken frustrations. Watching our father deteriorate was hard enough, but the strain it placed on our already fragile bond was something I hadn't anticipated.

By the time Dad passed, the rift between us felt permanent. Tracy stayed in Ibiza, continuing to live the life he had built there, while I remained here, rooted in my own. We don't talk anymore—not out of anger but because our lives are so vastly different that finding common ground seems impossible. He has his family, his spirituality, and his way of being, and I have mine.

There are moments when I miss what we could have had, the closeness that might have been if we'd been different people. But there's also a sense of acceptance. Not all siblings are destined to be best friends or even close. What we shared in childhood was enough—a bond built on shared roots, if not shared paths. In the end, he's still my brother, even if the connection now feels like a distant memory.

Sometimes, when I think of Tracy, I remember the early years before life pulled us in different directions. I see us as kids, running through the house, chasing after dreams neither of us could fully articulate. Those moments, though fleeting, remind me of a time when the differences didn't matter when being brothers was enough.

Looking back, I suppose the distance between us was always inevitable. Tracy and I were simply wired differently. While I thrived in environments that demanded energy, interaction, and an audience— whether on the rugby field or under the shadow of the Milky Bar Kid persona—Tracy was quieter, more introspective. He was the kind of person who didn't need the validation of a crowd, finding strength in solitude.

As we grew older, our differences manifested in the paths we chose. For me, life was about movement—sports, relationships, and the occasional creative outlet like my artwork. For Tracy, it was about discipline and personal growth. His commitment to bodybuilding was admirable; it became his identity, his way of navigating the world. I often wondered if it was his way of stepping out from under the shadow of being the younger brother, of finding a spotlight that was his alone.

But even then, there were moments of connection, however rare. I remember watching him compete in his early bodybuilding days, his focus unshakable as he prepared to step onto the stage. I admired his determination and the sheer willpower it took to sculpt himself into the best version of who he wanted to be. It was the same resolve I saw in myself when I trained for the London Marathon or tackled a rugby match. In those moments, I realized we weren't so different—we just channeled our energy in opposite directions.

Our father's passing, however, solidified the gap between us. When Dad fell ill, I felt an overwhelming sense of duty to be there, to support him through the long, difficult months. Tracy, living abroad, had a different perspective. His visits were sporadic, his approach to the situation pragmatic but detached. It was a stark contrast to my own emotional investment.

We clashed over decisions that had to be made—about care, about treatment, about how to handle the unrelenting march of time as our father's health declined. It was painful, not just because we disagreed but because those disagreements felt like another reminder of how far apart we'd grown.

By the time Dad passed in 2017, our already fragile bond had been worn thin, stretched to the point where there wasn't much left to hold onto, and then had been remolded into something that we both couldn't quite explain, far from what our relationship used to be before everything, but it was still something good, something that now when I remember, doesn't make me regret the last years of his life, which I'm so grateful for. Because my father may have been 87 when he passed but I saw that man got reduced to — a fragile being on prescribed bedrest from his illness. The same man who I had seen endure so much in his life with a strong head on his shoulders and a face that could brave any storm.

Tracy stayed in Ibiza after that, retreating further into the life he had built there. I remained here, trying to make sense of my own path without the anchor of our father's steady presence. The silence between us grew until it became the norm, an unspoken agreement that our lives were too different to reconcile.

Occasionally, I hear about him through mutual acquaintances or family updates. He's doing well, I'm told, happy in his spiritual pursuits and the rhythm of life he's carved out for himself. I wish him no ill will; in fact, I'm glad he's found a sense of peace. But it's hard not to feel a pang of regret for the relationship we might have had, the brotherhood that never quite took root in the way I'd hoped.

And yet, even as I reflect on the distance, I can't ignore the gratitude I feel for the shared history we do have. The laughter of childhood, the fleeting moments of understanding during our teenage years, and the lessons we've taught each other in the silence of adulthood—all of it has shaped who I am.

Life doesn't always give you the relationships you envision, but it gives you the ones you need to learn, to grow, and to reflect. Tracy and I may not walk the same path, but in our own ways, we've carried the essence of our shared past with us. Whether or not our paths ever cross again, I hope he knows that he's still my brother, and that's something that time or distance can never erase.

CHAPTER 6

THE INFLUENCE OF THE MILKY BAR KID ROLE

Being the Milky Bar Kid was a whirlwind, a chapter of my childhood that felt as surreal as it was exhilarating. At that age, I didn't fully understand the significance of the role. To me, it was just fun—dressing up in the iconic white shirt, red scarf, and cowboy hat, reciting my lines, and seeing the joy on people's faces. It felt like playing pretend but on a much grander scale, with cameras rolling and a team of adults guiding every move.

In those moments on set, I felt a sense of importance that was both thrilling and strange. Everyone listened to me, fussed over me, and made sure I was at the center of attention. For a child, that kind of recognition is intoxicating. I loved the applause, the way people's faces lit up when they realized who I was. Being the Milky Bar Kid gave me an identity, something that set me apart from other kids. I wasn't just a boy from the neighborhood—I was someone everyone knew.

But as much as I enjoyed the attention, it also set me apart in ways I didn't always understand. At school, I was no longer just another student. My classmates viewed me with a mix of admiration and curiosity, some eager to befriend "the kid from the adverts," while others kept their distance. I enjoyed the admiration but sometimes found myself wishing for the anonymity that other children seemed to take for granted.

The role also introduced me to a world of responsibility. Even though I was just a boy, I quickly learned that people expected me to behave a certain way, to live up to the cheerful, confident image of the Milky Bar Kid. It wasn't always easy to match that persona, especially on days when I didn't feel like smiling or being the center of attention. Still, I embraced the role wholeheartedly, proud of the uniqueness it brought to my life.

As I grew older, the Milky Bar Kid remained a part of my identity, even after my time in the role ended. People still recognized me, and the nickname followed me into my teenage years and beyond. It became a conversation starter, a connection to a past that people seemed to cherish as much as I did. Yet, there were times when I felt confined by it as if that role was all anyone saw of me.

The experience shaped my aspirations in subtle but lasting ways. It taught me the value of confidence and presence, of stepping into a space and owning it. It also gave me an early understanding of how identity can be both a gift and a challenge. I carried the Milky Bar Kid with me into every new venture, from sports to art, letting it remind me that standing out was a strength.

Looking back now, I can see how the Milky Bar Kid gave me more than just a moment in the spotlight—it gave me the foundation to build on as I navigated life's opportunities and challenges. It's a part of me I'll always cherish, not just for the fame it brought but for the lessons it taught me about embracing who you are, even when the world sees you through a single lens.

Even as the years passed and the role faded from the public eye, its impact on my life remained undeniable. It became more than a chapter of my childhood; it was a thread woven into the fabric of who I was becoming. The Milky Bar Kid had given me a glimpse of a world beyond my own, a world filled with possibilities I might never have considered otherwise.

As a teenager, I began to realize how deeply the experience had shaped my sense of self. It wasn't just the recognition or the occasional "Weren't you the Milky Bar Kid?" that followed me wherever I went. It was the confidence the role had instilled in me. Standing in front of a camera, delivering lines, and embodying a character had taught me to carry myself with assurance. It was a skill I carried with me into new challenges, whether on the rugby pitch, at school, or even later in my career.

However, being the Milky Bar Kid also brought its share of challenges. There were moments when I felt like I had to live up to the cheerful, heroic image of the character, even when I didn't feel that way inside.

It was as if the persona had set a benchmark for who I was supposed to be. Sometimes, I wondered if people truly saw me or just the boy from the adverts. That question lingered in the back of my mind as I navigated friendships, school, and the inevitable awkwardness of growing up.

The role also sparked an early understanding of how fleeting the spotlight could be. By the time I was no longer the Milky Bar Kid, I was still adjusting to what life looked like without the constant buzz of cameras and attention. It was a strange transition, going from being the center of the world to just another face in the crowd. But in that shift, I found a certain freedom—a chance to discover who I was beyond the character I'd played.

The influence of the Milky Bar Kid extended far beyond those childhood years. It shaped my outlook on life, giving me a unique perspective on identity and the power of storytelling. I often found myself reflecting on the balance between the public persona and the person I was inside. Those reflections informed many of the choices I made, from my passion for art to my love of sports, and even the way I approached relationships.

Even now, when people mention the Milky Bar Kid, I feel a mix of pride and nostalgia. It's a reminder of a time when life felt larger than life when anything seemed possible. But more than that, it's a reminder of the lessons I've carried with me—the confidence to stand out, the resilience to navigate expectations, and the joy of embracing a role that became a cornerstone of my story.

The Milky Bar Kid wasn't just a character I played; it was a defining part of my journey. It taught me to step into the spotlight and, more importantly, to carry that light with me, even long after the cameras stopped rolling.

PART – III
PERSONAL CHALLENGES AND TRIUMPHS

CHAPTER 7

FAMILY STRUGGLES AND LOSS

Life is rarely a straight path. It twists and turns, sometimes leading us into places we never imagined—some filled with light, others shadowed by sorrow. For me, the greatest trials came not from the challenges I faced as a child or even the struggles of growing up, but from the losses that cut into the very fabric of my existence. Some wounds never fully heal, and some names remain etched in the heart forever.

The Strength of My Mother: Dolly's Final Lessons

Similarly, there are moments in life that define you, that shape who you are in ways you never expected. Losing my mother was one of those moments.

My mother, Dolly, was everything to me—warm, strong, and full of life. She had a way of making people feel safe, of turning even the hardest days into something bearable. She wasn't just my mother; she was my greatest inspiration. And then, in 1978, when she was only 50, we got the news that shattered everything—cancer. Ovarian. The doctors didn't sugarcoat it. They gave her little time.

I was devastated. We all were. But somehow, she wasn't. She came home, not to fight, but to spend whatever time she had left surrounded by us—her family. We moved her bed into our lounge, where my father, my brother, and I could be with her as much as possible. I watched, helpless, as the disease took its toll, stealing her strength, her hair, her body. Her spine twisted, and her frame grew frail, but her spirit never did.

There were nights when I would climb into bed beside her, just to hold her, to try and keep her here a little longer. I knew she was in pain, but she never let it define her. She still smiled, still gave me the kind of love that only a mother can give. And in the quiet moments, she spoke truths that I didn't fully understand at the time.

31

A week before she died, she looked at me—really looked at me—and said, "Son, your life is going to be very hard... but you must endure."

I didn't know what she meant then. I thought I did, but I didn't. Not yet.

She passed away on April 2nd, 1979, just a day after I turned 23. She was 51. And though I had known it was coming, nothing could have prepared me for the emptiness that followed.

Grief doesn't announce itself. It just moves in, silently, rearranging your entire world. I carried my mother's words with me, even when I didn't want to. Because she was right. Life would be hard. I would face losses I never could have imagined. But I would endure. Because that's what she taught me to do.

Meeting Hayley: Young Love and Early Foundations

Before life taught me about heartache and resilience, it first introduced me to young love. I was just eighteen years old—a tough lad on the football and rugby field, but still very much a novice when it came to girls. She knew of me before I even knew her. Back then, in Canvey Island in 1974, the name "Milky" carried weight long before I ever understood why.

We met in a local nightclub. I still remember that night—her presence commanded the room. Hayley was stunning. A dancer with poise and energy that made her unforgettable. She later became a dance teacher, and it was clear from the start that she carried a grace and discipline I admired deeply. We dated for five years, young and hopeful, and married in 1979. Life seemed simple then, full of promise.

Brooke arrived in 1982, followed by Raine in 1984, and I thought I had everything. A wife, two beautiful daughters, and a future stretching out before me. But life has a way of changing course. After seven years of marriage, Hayley wanted out. In 1986, she left, and I found myself standing at a crossroads I never anticipated—alone with two young girls, holding full custody, and no choice but to carry on.

Custody of My Daughters: A New Chapter After a Breakup

When you become a parent, the world shifts. Suddenly, your own needs become secondary, and every decision, every sacrifice, is made with the well-being of your children in mind. My daughters were my world, the center of everything I did, and when my relationship with their mother ended, the transition was anything but easy.

Breakups are painful, but when children are involved, they carry an even heavier weight. There's no clean break, no simple way to walk away, because no matter how fractured a relationship becomes, the love for your children remains intact. The custody battle wasn't just about legalities—it was about proving to myself and to the world that I could be the father my daughters needed.

Routines changed, emotions ran high, and there were nights when the silence in the house felt unbearable. I had spent years envisioning a life where my family was whole, but now I was standing in a new reality, one where I had to navigate fatherhood in a different way. I had to be strong, even when I felt like breaking. I had to be present, even when the weight of the past tried to pull me under.

Somehow, we found our rhythm. Love, I realized, wasn't about circumstances—it was about consistency. No matter what had happened between their mother and me, my daughters would always have a father who showed up, who fought for them, and who loved them beyond words.

The Tragic Death of Raine

But nothing in life could have prepared me for the day I lost Raine.

Some moments divide life into *before* and *after*, and that was one of them. A phone call. A moment of disbelief. And then the crushing reality that my child—my Raine—was gone.

I still remember every detail of that day. It was hot, the summer heat blistering in the afternoon. The kids were playing outside in the front yard, while I worked on something in the kitchen with the front door open. I remember the joyful screams of the kids turning into panicked and anxious ones as they called out to me.

I still remember how my heart had stopped seeing Raine missing from the number of heads in front of me, all safe. All safe but Raine.

Looking around, she had just been sitting behind a car at the end of the road on the other side, nothing too big or too out of the ordinary for wandering kids. But my heart had lurched into my throat the moment she had started moving after seeing me. And despite my firm and poorly veiled panicked call of "Stay there!" she had not stayed.

The moment she had seen her father, she was on the move towards me, and perhaps that was my own mistake for calling my own kid's attention to myself when she was in a situation so unknown and uncertain for her.

What came after was not anyone else's fault, despite the fact that I wanted to blame it on someone just to ease the pain, to make the constraints around my lungs, around my heart, and my throat loosen up. Just so I could breathe through the sudden wave of sorrow that washed over me as I held Raine's small body in my arms. So small, so full of curiosity and hope and all good things that she had yet to learn of the future.

All gone. In an instant.

I had seen her getting hit by a car, right in front of me. The moment itself was one that would forever be ingrained in my mind, in my heart, and in my soul.

People talk about grief as if it's a process, something with defined stages, something you can move through. But when it's your own child, it's not a process—it's a storm, relentless and unyielding. The news hit like a wrecking ball, shattering everything I thought I knew about pain.

Raine had been full of life, a spirit so vibrant it was impossible to imagine a world without them in it. And yet, suddenly, that world existed—a world where Raine's laughter was now a memory, where the plans we had made would never come to pass.

I don't remember much from the days that followed. They blurred together in a haze of disbelief and unbearable sorrow. I would wake up each morning, hoping it had been a nightmare, only to be met with the same crushing truth. The world outside continued on as if nothing had changed, while mine had crumbled into dust.

34

I struggled with the *why* of it all. Why Raine? Why now? Why this? No answer ever came, and maybe that's the cruelest part of grief—the way it leaves you with questions that will never be answered.

Ongoing Grief: A Love That Never Fades

People often talk about *moving on*, but I've learned that grief doesn't work that way. You don't move on—you move forward, carrying the loss with you, letting it shape you in ways you never wanted but can't deny.

At the time, the only thing that kept me going was the thought of Brooke. Little, innocent Brooke, who didn't even know what losing a sister, and losing Raine had meant. So young, that I had to sit down and explain to her that her precious play-buddy, her ever-ready partner in all the quiet shenanigans was now gone, forever.

The absence of Raine not only impacted me but also Brooke as well. It not only shook the basis of her childhood but also any hope for a stable relationship she might have had with the ones around her. She grew up to be an angry teenager, angry at the world, angry at me, angry at the fact that life had taken something so precious from her so early on.

It fractured the relationship we had, so much so that she had moved out of our house and lodged with other people she trusted enough to live with. Maybe it was because she needed space from all the reminders of Raine that were still present in our house, maybe seeing me visibly mourn and grieve on my bad days, made it difficult for her to move on.

For whatever reason, I never pushed her.

And maybe that was for the better because I didn't believe in the saying, "Distance makes the heart grow fonder," until I experienced it myself. Maybe it's not true for a lot of people, but for me and my kid, it worked.

Eventually, we gathered all the fractured pieces of our relationship and put them back together into something resembling a normal father-daughter relationship, which grew into a much beautiful and stable bond over the years. Especially, when Dexter, her precious son, was brought into our lives.

But despite it all, Raine's memory is still woven into the fabric of my life.

I see them in the quiet moments, in the songs that remind me of their laughter, in the spaces they once filled. Some days, the grief is gentle, like a whisper. Other days, it's a tidal wave, knocking me off my feet when I least expect it.

But through it all, I hold onto one thing: love. Because if grief is the price we pay for love, then I will carry it gladly. Raine was, and always will be, a part of me.

There are no words to fully capture the depth of that loss, just as there are no words to describe the love that remains. But if Raine's life taught me anything, it's that love doesn't end—it transforms. And so, I keep moving, not away from the grief, but with it, carrying Raine with me in every step, in every breath, in every moment of this life that continues.

The Empty Space That Never Fills

Losing Raine wasn't just losing a person—it was losing a part of myself, a piece of my soul that could never be replaced. The silence they left behind was deafening. There were days when I would wake up expecting to hear their voice, only to be met with the crushing quiet. I would catch myself wanting to tell them something, a joke, a thought, a memory, only to realize that those conversations would now only happen in my mind.

People say time heals, but they don't tell you that healing doesn't mean forgetting. It doesn't mean the pain disappears. It just means you learn to live with the ache, like a scar that never quite fades. Raine is still here, in the spaces they used to fill, in the laughter that echoes in my memory, in the way the world feels a little dimmer without them.

The Strength to Keep Going

At first, I didn't know how to move forward. There were days when getting out of bed felt impossible when the weight of grief pressed so hard against my chest that I wondered how I was still breathing. But I kept going because that's what Raine would have wanted. They would have wanted me to keep living, to keep loving, to find joy even in the pain.

I turned to the things that grounded me—my daughters, my art, my memories. I found solace in the routine of life, in the simple acts of waking up, making coffee, going for walks. I learned that grief doesn't have to be an enemy; it can be a reminder. A reminder of the love that existed, of the bond that can never be broken.

Some days, the memories are enough to bring a smile to my face. Other days, they bring tears. And that's okay. That's the nature of love—it doesn't fade just because the person is gone. It lingers, it weaves itself into the fabric of who we are.

Honoring Raine's Memory

These days, I see Raine's silhouette in my grandson, Dexter. The way he plays, the way he calls to his mother. It's hard some days when the memory of Raine echoes in every corner of the house. But then come the days that his presence makes the absence of Raine lighter.

Maybe the same is the case for Brooke, maybe it isn't, regardless, I'm grateful to her for bringing Dexter into our lives. Perhaps, it's not fair of me to say this, but I wait for him to grow old and see how much of Raine reflects in him and how much of his own person he becomes.

Because I knew I couldn't change what happened, but I could choose how I carried Raine's memory forward. So I did. I spoke about them. I kept their spirit alive in the stories I told, in the lessons they taught me, in the love that still exists between us.

Every year, on the day Raine left this world, I take a moment to honor them. I light a candle. I sit in the quiet. I let myself feel everything— love, pain, gratitude, sorrow. I remind myself that grief is just love with nowhere to go, and I send that love out into the world, hoping that, somehow, Raine feels it.

I see them in the little things—a song on the radio, the way the sky looks before a storm, the way the wind carries whispers of something unseen. I like to believe they are still here, watching over me, guiding me in ways I may never fully understand.

A Love That Never Ends

There will never be a day when I stop missing Raine. There will never be a moment when their absence doesn't weigh on me. But there will also never be a day when I stop loving them.

Grief is not the end of the story. It is a chapter in the book of love, a chapter that continues to unfold, even as the years pass. Raine's life, though shorter than it should have been, was full of meaning, full of light. And that light, no matter how much time passes, will never go out.

In 1990, a few years after losing Raine to that terrible, terrible accident, I decided to run the London Marathon. At the time, it had felt important for me to do something that would preserve her memory. So, I raised money for the kids of Great Ormond Street Hospital, hoping to give an opportunity to those who were fighting their own battles. Running and completing the marathon was a personal challenge, and knowing I was making a difference, and saving lives, made it even more meaningful.

So I keep going, not because the pain has faded, but because the love remains. And in that love, Raine lives on.

CHAPTER 8

A NEW CHAPTER WITH VIOLETTA

Life has a way of surprising you when you least expect it. Just when you think you've seen all its twists and turns, it throws something—or someone—into your path who changes everything. For me, that someone was Violetta.

Meeting Violi: A Chance Encounter at Sea

We met in September 2004, aboard a cruise ship weaving its way through the serene waters around the Seychelles and Zanzibar. I was a guest, seeking respite and perhaps a spark of connection. She was a masseuse from the Philippines, exuding warmth and grace that seemed to draw people in. There was a certain charm to her—a gentleness in her manner and a soft kindness in her smile. Conversations came easily, and before long, I found myself captivated by the promise of what could be.

A Quick Marriage, a Hopeful Beginning

Just four months later, we were married in the Philippines. At the time, it felt right. After years of heartache and loneliness, I craved love, companionship, and stability. I told myself that sometimes, love moves quickly, and perhaps happiness didn't have to be complicated. But in hindsight, I see the signs I chose to ignore.

Settling in England: Doubts and Denial

After navigating the bureaucratic maze of visa requirements, Violy arrived in England with her two sons around ten months after we first met. The early days carried hope. We adjusted built routines and tried to merge our lives. But slowly, cracks began to show. Words left unspoken, glances that avoided meeting mine, and moments of cold detachment became impossible to overlook. Still, I pushed forward. I had been through heartbreak before and refused to believe I was facing it again.

An Inevitable Ending

For years, we jogged along, ignoring the tension simmering beneath the surface. But in July 2012, the inevitable happened—Violy left. Her youngest son, Anthony, just 15 at the time, chose to stay with me. His presence was a small comfort in a time of growing despair.

The Weight of Collapse

The months that followed were among the darkest of my life. By September 2012, the pressure became unbearable. My spirit, once so resilient, finally crumbled. I was admitted and sectioned into the mental health department at Basildon Hospital. Six long months passed, where I struggled to piece myself back together and find clarity in the chaos.

Finding Purpose in the Darkness

This breakdown was triggered not just by the weight of life's mounting challenges, but by the collapse of my second marriage, and Violy's relentless, ruthless pursuit of money. All my old troubles came flooding back, compounding the strain. Stepping into the hospital September felt like walking into the unknown. I couldn't help but think of *One Flew Over the Cuckoo's Nest*, fearing what lay ahead.

The first six weeks were the hardest — adjusting to this unfamiliar, sometimes hostile, and often deeply sad place. I kept to myself at first, unsure and wary. But gradually, I began to engage with the staff and other patients. Before long, I found myself becoming somewhat of a spokesman — not just for myself, but for others who couldn't always speak for themselves. I wanted to help however I could: stepping in to defuse tensions, stopping fights (I'm a strong little fella), aiding the elderly, and supporting anyone who needed a hand. This community became, in many ways, my family, and I did everything I could to care for them.

My efforts didn't go unnoticed. Dr. Ghaniker, the head consultant overseeing my care, took note. When I was discharged in April 2013, after nearly seven months, he wrote me a remarkable letter describing how he'd witnessed my compassion and willingness to help those less able. He encouraged me to carry that passion forward, to do something with it — something bigger.

While this time was heartbreaking, I believe it shaped me into who I am today. It gave me a new mindset, a deeper strength I didn't know I possessed — one I would desperately need. Because the moment I left the hospital, Violy was back at it, showing little empathy for what I'd endured. But I stood firm. I endured.

My property—purchased and secured long before she entered my life—hung in the balance. The home I had built with my own hands and sacrifices was under threat.

Hard-Fought Victories

In the end, I managed to keep my home, but not without great cost. I was forced to part with money I felt she had no right to claim. She had never contributed financially, never invested in building what I had. And yet, she walked away with more than she deserved.

Reflecting on Her True Intentions

Looking back, I can't help but ask myself: Did she have a plan from the very beginning? Was it all about the visa, the financial security, the comfort built on my years of hard work? I will never truly know the full extent of her intentions, but the pieces now fit together in ways they never did before.

The Lesson Left Behind

Violy's place in my story was not that of a partner but a teacher of hard lessons. She taught me that not every connection is genuine, that trust must be earned with time, and that love without sincerity is merely convenience dressed up in affection. But even in loss, I found resilience. I learned to rebuild from the wreckage, to protect what mattered most, and to trust in myself when others fail. And perhaps, in the end, that was the lesson I was meant to carry forward.

PART – IV
ADVENTURES AROUND
THE WORLD

CHAPTER 9

TRAVELS AND EXPLORATIONS

There's something about travel that transforms you. It stretches the mind, challenges the familiar, and reminds you that the world is vast beyond comprehension. For me, travel has never been just about visiting new places — it's been about experiencing life in all its color, rhythm, and unpredictability. Every journey has left an imprint on me, subtly shaping who I am and how I see the world.

I've been fortunate — blessed, really — to have traveled to over 160 countries, touching every continent and setting foot in every corner of Europe, from the grandest capitals to the tiniest principalities. Each place, no matter how large or small, has told its own story. Different cultures, different landscapes, different values, and different experiences—each one unique, each one unforgettable.

Early Travel Experiences: Vancouver and Canada

One of my first significant travel experiences took me to Vancouver, Canada. At the time, I didn't quite know what to expect. I had seen pictures and heard stories, but nothing could compare to standing there in the crisp Canadian air, surrounded by landscapes that felt almost too vast to be real.

Vancouver was a city that seemed to have it all — towering mountains, a sparkling coastline, and an energy that was both vibrant and laid-back at the same time. I remember walking along the harbor, taking in the sight of seaplanes gliding across the water, their engines humming against the backdrop of the city skyline.

But beyond the beauty of the place, what struck me most was the people. Canadians, as I quickly learned, were some of the warmest, most welcoming people I had ever met. Whether it was a simple conversation in a café or a shared laugh with a stranger, there was a kindness in them that made me feel at home, even so far away from everything familiar.

Memorable Trips: Colombia, the Trans-Siberian Express, Moscow, and Tibet

As I continued to explore the world, my travels took me to places I never thought I'd see — places filled with history, culture, and stories waiting to be told.

Colombia was unlike anywhere I had ever been before. The energy of the cities, the music that seemed to pulse through the streets, the stunning landscapes that stretched from jungles to beaches — it was a country of contrasts, and I loved every second of it. I remember sitting in a small café, watching the world go by, sipping on some of the best coffee I had ever tasted. Colombia was raw, real, and alive in a way that few places are.

One day while relaxing at a local pool in Colombia, I found myself watching a man who couldn't be ignored. He was a Black guy, sitting coolly in the water, sunglasses on, heavy chains hanging from his neck, and surrounded by stunning women. He noticed me watching, and with a big grin, called out, "Hey, man, you like my ladies?" I laughed nervously, "No, I'm okay, thank you."

"Where you from, man?" he asked. "The UK," I replied. At that, his smile grew wider. "You want to come with me and my ladies for the day?" he offered. I politely declined again.

As he turned back to his entourage, I felt a wave of relief. He certainly reminded me of a cartel drug baron, and I couldn't help but think— well, at least he didn't shoot me.

Then came the **Trans-Siberian Express**, a journey that was as much about the experience as it was about the destination. There's something mesmerizing about traveling by train, watching the world shift outside your window, and feeling the rhythm of the tracks beneath you. The journey was long, spanning across Russia's vast landscapes, from bustling cities to remote villages where life seemed untouched by time.

Arriving in **Moscow**, I was met with a city of grandeur and history. The Red Square, with its imposing Kremlin walls and the colorful domes of St. Basil's Cathedral, felt like stepping into a postcard. But what fascinated me most about Moscow wasn't just its beauty — it was its depth. Beneath the surface of its majestic architecture and bustling streets, there was a history that spoke of resilience, of a people who had seen war, revolution, and rebirth.

Then there was **Tibet**, a place that felt almost otherworldly. The moment I arrived, I understood why so many travelers spoke of its spiritual energy. The towering peaks of the Himalayas, the quiet hum of monks chanting in distant monasteries, the prayer flags fluttering in the wind—it all felt sacred, untouched.

One of my most vivid memories from Tibet was visiting the **Potala Palace**, a structure that seemed to defy gravity, perched high above the city of Lhasa. Walking through its ancient halls, I could feel the weight of history around me. The stories of past Dalai Lamas, of political struggles and spiritual awakenings, seemed to echo in every corner.

Highlights: Unique Experiences and Personal Reflections

Every trip brought with it moments of wonder, moments that I still carry with me.

In Canada, it was the awe of nature, the feeling of standing at the edge of a vast wilderness and realizing just how small we are in the grand scheme of things.

In Colombia, it was the rhythm of life, the music, the passion of the people, and the way the streets felt alive with movement and color.

On the Trans-Siberian journey, it was the solitude, the quiet reflection that comes with watching the landscape change outside a train window, and the realization that sometimes, the journey itself is more important than the destination.

In Moscow, it was the weight of history, the understanding that cities are built not just of stone and steel, but of stories, of triumphs and tragedies that shape their people.

And in Tibet, it was peace — the kind of peace that only comes from being in a place where time seems to move differently, where the world slows down just enough for you to truly see it.

Travel, for me, has never been about checking places off a list. It's about the experiences, the people, the moments that leave a lasting impression. Every place I've been has given me something — whether it was a new perspective, a deepened appreciation, or simply a memory that will stay with me forever.

And as long as I live, I will keep seeking those moments. Because the world is too big, too beautiful, to stay in one place for too long.

The Soul of a Traveler

Travel is more than just movement—it's transformation. With every new place I visited, I carried back something intangible: a lesson, a feeling, a story. The world was my classroom, and each destination left its mark, shaping me into the person I am today. Some journeys stood out more than others, and some moments remain etched in my mind as if they happened yesterday.

A Walk Through History in Moscow

Moscow was more than a city; it was a living, breathing history book. Walking through **Red Square**, I felt as though I had stepped into the pages of a grand epic. The **Kremlin** loomed with an air of authority, its red walls enclosing centuries of political power. **St. Basil's Cathedral**, with its vibrant, swirling domes, looked almost too magical to be real, like something out of a dream.

Yet, Moscow wasn't just about its famous landmarks. It was the feeling of standing in a place where history had unfolded, where leaders had risen and fallen, where revolutions had been born. There was an energy to it, a quiet power that whispered of resilience.

One of the moments that struck me most was riding the **Moscow Metro**. It wasn't just a transport system—it was an underground palace. The stations, adorned with chandeliers, mosaics, and marble columns, were unlike anything I had ever seen. It was a reminder that even in the most ordinary of places, beauty could be found.

Through the Vastness of Siberia

The **Trans-Siberian Railway** was a journey of patience and wonder. There's something meditative about watching the landscape shift from the window of a moving train. From the dense forests of Russia's heartland to the snow-covered plains of Siberia, every mile told a different story.

Life on the train was simple. Days blurred into nights as we rolled across the country. Conversations with strangers became the highlight of the trip—people from all walks of life, sharing meals, stories, and laughter. There was an unspoken bond among travelers, a shared understanding that we were all just passing through, both on the train and in life.

One evening, as the sun dipped below the horizon, painting the sky in shades of orange and purple, I sat by the window, lost in thought. I realized how small I was in the grand scheme of things, just another traveler on a journey that had been taken by thousands before me and would be taken by thousands after. And yet, in that moment, it felt uniquely mine.

The Spiritual Heights of Tibet

Tibet was unlike any place I had ever been. It was as if the very air carried wisdom as if the mountains themselves whispered secrets of an ancient past.

The **Potala Palace**, once the home of the Dalai Lama, stood high above Lhasa, a fortress of faith and history. Climbing its countless steps, I felt a sense of reverence. Inside, the scent of burning incense filled the air, and the walls were lined with statues, scriptures, and golden relics. The monks, draped in deep red robes, moved with quiet grace, their chants echoing through the halls.

But the most profound moment came not in a grand temple, but in a small monastery tucked away in the mountains. There, I met an elderly monk who had spent decades in quiet meditation. His face was lined with age, but his eyes held a kindness and peace that I had never seen before.

We didn't speak the same language, but somehow, words weren't necessary. In his presence, I felt an overwhelming sense of calm—a reminder that peace isn't found in places, but within ourselves.

The Wild Heart of Colombia

If Tibet was serenity, **Colombia** was pure, untamed energy. The streets pulsed with music, the air was thick with the scent of spices and fresh fruit, and the people carried a passion for life that was contagious.

I wandered through **Cartagena**, a city where the walls told stories, their vibrant colors reflecting the spirit of its people. The old town, with its colonial architecture and cobbled streets, felt like a step back in time. But beyond the beauty, what struck me most was the resilience of the people.

Colombia had seen its share of hardship, yet its people refused to be defined by struggle. They danced, they laughed, they lived with an intensity that was inspiring.

One evening, as I sat in a small café, watching the world go by, a local musician began to play. The melody was rich, full of sorrow and joy intertwined. And in that moment, I understood something: Colombia wasn't just a place—it was a feeling, an emotion, a testament to the human spirit.

Though each place has left its mark, some destinations stand apart, etched in my memory for what they revealed about the world — and about me.

Japan: Tradition and Tranquility

Japan captivated me with its balance of ancient tradition and cutting-edge modernity. Temples sat quietly amidst bustling cities, and the care with which every detail of daily life was handled spoke to generations of respect and refinement. Walking through Tokyo in the early morning mist, I felt as though I had stepped into a dream.

New Zealand: Nature's Masterpiece

New Zealand felt like nature showing off. Majestic mountains met rolling green fields, pristine lakes mirrored skies so pure they felt unreal. It was wild, beautiful, and grounding all at once.

Antarctica: The Last Untouched Place

Antarctica, by contrast, was purity itself. Towering icebergs, endless silence, and air so clean it felt like breathing the beginning of the world.

The landscape was humbling, a reminder of how fragile and beautiful this planet can be.

India: Chaotic Wonder

India was chaos in its most beautiful form. Colorful, loud, overwhelming — every sense was constantly engaged. The clash of ancient and modern, the spiritual and the mundane, created an energy I've found nowhere else. It wasn't always easy, but it was always alive.

Scotland: Humor and Heart

Scotland, with its rugged landscapes and mysterious lochs, felt like a smaller, cheekier version of New Zealand. The humor and banter, the friendly rivalry with England, the warmth of its people — it all combined with stunning scenery to create a place that felt like an old friend.

Reflections on the Road

Looking back, I realize that travel was never about escape—it was about discovery. Not just of new places, but of myself. Every journey added a layer to my understanding of the world, each experience leaving behind a lesson.

In Moscow, I learned that history is alive, and woven into the fabric of a city and its people.

On the Trans-Siberian Railway, I learned the value of patience, of letting go and simply enjoying the journey.

In Tibet, I found a deeper understanding of inner peace, a reminder that the world's greatest lessons often come in silence.

And in Colombia, I discovered the power of resilience, of living life with passion, despite its hardships.

Japan showed me grace and precision.

New Zealand displayed nature in its purest form.

Antarctica humbled me with its untouched beauty.

India taught me to embrace chaos and find joy in unpredictability.

Scotland reminded me that humor and warmth can make anywhere feel like home.

Travel has been my teacher. The world — its landscapes, cultures, and people — has shown me how vast, varied, and beautiful life can be. And though I've seen more of it than most — over 160 countries, each leaving its mark — I know there's still more to learn, more to feel, more to understand.

The world is vast, filled with wonders waiting to be seen, stories waiting to be heard. And as long as I have breath in my lungs, I will keep exploring, keep learning, and keep seeking those moments that remind me just how incredible this life truly is.

CHAPTER 10

ENCOUNTERS AND REFLECTIONS

Travel isn't just about seeing new places—it's about the people you meet, the experiences that shape you, and the unexpected moments that leave you breathless. Some journeys are about adventure, others about introspection. But the ones that stay with you forever are the ones that remind you of the raw, untamed beauty of the world and the people who call it home.

Uganda: The Hippo That Didn't Care

I went to Uganda thinking I'd feel something deep. Maybe I'd cry. Maybe something in me would shift. You imagine wild gorillas and thick forests, and suddenly you're some poetic version of yourself.

But the truth is, Uganda was... quiet. And weird. Not weird-bad. Weird-true.

One evening, I stood by the edge of a lake. The light was gone. Everything was blue and grey. And then I saw it — a hippo. Just its eyes and ears above water. It didn't move. It didn't flinch. It didn't care that I was there, or that I was looking. It just... was.

And I remember thinking, *"This thing has figured it out."*

No social performance. No storytelling. No "look at me, I'm wild and majestic." It wasn't trying to inspire awe or win a National Geographic feature. It was just being. Unbothered. Heavy and still and whole.

I must've stood there for an hour. I didn't take pictures. Didn't speak. Just watched. And for the first time in a long time, I felt — not small — but irrelevant. Not in a bad way. Just... out of the frame.

And when it finally sank back under the water, like some ancient god disappearing without fanfare, I laughed.

Not because it was funny. But because it was real.

I thought seeing gorillas would break something open in me. But it was the hippo that did it. It was so wildly indifferent to my presence that I

51

finally stopped performing too. I just stood there, still — human, yes, but also something more honest than that.

"When you get what you want, you don't want what you got."

That line hit me later. Not in disappointment, but in realignment.

Turkey: Rain, Ruins, and an Empty Mosque

Before I even made it into Istanbul, I had a strange encounter at the airport.

I got stopped at customs. Confident as ever, I stepped forward and said, "Hi, I'm Milky Harris—is there a problem?"

The officer stared at me flatly. "Are you carrying drugs?"

"No," I replied, confused.

"We need to search you. Take your shirt off."

I hesitated, feeling my stomach twist. "Drop your shorts," came the next order—this time, harsher.

I was seriously crapping myself now. Voice quivering, I said, "I've no drugs, sir." But they just repeated it: "Drop your shorts."

As I began to lower them, the officers burst into laughter. "On your way, Milky Harris."

Gosh, that was a relief. They'd done me like a kipper. In hindsight, it was hilarious. At the time? Not so much.

I didn't go to Turkey chasing anything. I just wanted silence. Istanbul was loud, but under the noise, there was something ancient humming. You could feel it in the bricks.

One morning it rained. Not pouring, just this soft, indecisive drizzle. I ducked into a mosque — one of the small ones, not the tourist showpieces. No one was there. Not even a caretaker. Just me, the carpets, the echo of something older than memory.

I didn't pray. I didn't speak. I just sat.

I had been walking all morning — no destination, just drifting — and my feet ached. But it wasn't just that. My thoughts were loud. Loud in that useless way, where you're trying to make sense of things that won't make sense. And in that space, in that hush, I remember thinking:

"This is it. This is what I needed. A room without expectation."

No calligraphies were screaming meaning at me. No guided reflections. Just four walls and air that felt like it had waited a long time to be noticed.

When the rain stopped, I stood up and left. Nothing changed. And maybe that was the change.

Colombia: The Old Man and the Rain

Colombia wasn't loud for me. It was hushed. Every night, the streets of Bogotá felt like they were holding something they didn't want to share.

I remember one evening — it had rained, not hard, but just enough to make the stones shine. I walked with no plan, just letting the city carry me. And I saw him. An old man, standing outside a closed barbershop. He had one hand behind his back, the other holding a cigarette that wasn't lit.

We didn't speak. He didn't nod. He didn't ask for anything. He just watched me. Not in a threatening way. Not in a friendly way. Just... present.

I crossed the street and kept walking. But I couldn't shake him. Not because of who he was, but because of what he wasn't — a distraction, a label, a story.

That's the thing. In Colombia, I stopped needing things to be meaningful. Sometimes they just are.

Later that night, I sat by a broken streetlight, listening to dogs fight in the distance, and I thought,

"Maybe the mystery isn't something to solve. Maybe it's something to sit with."

Philadelphia: That Subway Stare

Philly was cold that day. Not weather-cold—something else. The kind of cold that hums in your chest.

I was riding the subway, standing near the doors. It was late, and the carriage was mostly empty. A man sat across from me. Heavy coat. Eyes like he'd already seen what I hadn't.

He didn't move. Didn't blink. Just watched me.

And I wasn't afraid. Not exactly. But something in me froze.

There was no violence in him. No threat. Just this deep, silent knowing — like he saw something in me I hadn't figured out yet.

I got off two stops early. Didn't look back.

That moment stuck. Not because anything happened. But because nothing did. And still, I walked out of that train feeling like a part of me stayed behind.

Reflections on a Life Well-Traveled

From the depths of the Ugandan jungle to the bustling streets of Turkey, from the cold landscapes of Russia to the warm hearts of Philadelphia's homeless, I've come to understand one thing—**the world is full of stories**.

Some stories make you laugh, some break your heart, and some leave you in awe of the sheer beauty of existence.

One moment in Thailand touched me in a way I didn't expect. I was walking through a market with an American friend who lived there when we passed a stall selling frogs—bags of them, still alive.

To my surprise, my friend bought the whole lot. I assumed he planned to cook them. But instead, he drove us to a nearby lake, carried the bag to the edge of the water, and let them go. Some were already dead, but a few slipped into the lake and swam free.

"If I can save just a few, it's worth it," he said.

That moment hit me. If you can help even one life—even if most can't be saved—then you've done something meaningful. That, to me, is the true test of being human.

I've danced in places where I didn't know the language. I've shared meals with strangers who became friends. I've stood face-to-face with creatures that reminded me of our shared connection to the natural world. And through it all, I've learned that we are all, in some way, travelers—searching for meaning, for connection, for moments that remind us why we are alive.

And so, I keep moving, keep exploring, keep collecting stories—not just for myself, but for the people who may never get the chance to see what I have seen. Because in the end, the greatest adventure isn't the places we visit, but the lives we touch along the way.

The Stories That Stay With You

Travel is never just about the places—it's about the moments, the people, and the emotions they leave behind. Some journeys gift you with pure adventure, some teach you humility, and some force you to confront the fragility of life itself. But no matter where I've gone, there are experiences that have stayed with me, woven into the fabric of who I am.

The Silent Connection: A Second Encounter with Uganda's Gorillas

My first time seeing the **mountain gorillas of Uganda** had been a breathtaking moment, but my second visit was something different altogether—deeper, more profound. I returned to **Bwindi Impenetrable Forest**, hoping to relive the magic of that first encounter. What I didn't expect was an experience that would stay with me forever.

This time, we had been trekking for hours with no sign of the gorillas. The forest was alive with sounds—chirping birds, rustling leaves, distant hoots of unseen primates—but the group was growing weary. Then, just as hope began to wane, a rustle in the bushes brought us all to a standstill.

A young gorilla, no older than two or three, emerged, its dark eyes filled with curiosity. Slowly, cautiously, it stepped closer. I held my breath, feeling the group around me freeze, caught in the awe of the moment. Then, in a gesture that took my breath away, the young gorilla reached out, its tiny fingers brushing against my boot before scampering back into the undergrowth.

It was just a second—a fleeting, delicate moment—but it was everything. A silent connection, a reminder that despite our differences, there is something universal that ties all life together.

But not everything was so gentle. During that second trip, I got too close to a silverback, while trying to take pictures.

We had been warned to be still and respectful if they approached—but in my excitement, I didn't see the danger.

Suddenly, this huge silverback rushed me. It all happened so fast—I couldn't move in time. It slammed into my stomach and I went down, completely winded. My group stared in shock, mouths agape.

Later, one of the guides said, "You were in his way. That was just a tap. If he wanted to kill you, you'd be dead."

It's funny to reflect on now. I figure, if I could take a hit from a silverback gorilla, I could probably take one from Mike Tyson too.

An Unexpected Lesson in Patience: Lost in a Tibetan Village

Not all my experiences were wrapped in beauty and wonder. Some were downright frustrating—like the time I got **hopelessly lost in Tibet**.

I had been exploring a small village outside of Lhasa, wandering through narrow alleyways, drawn in by the scent of burning incense and the rhythmic chanting of monks. I wasn't worried at first. I had a map, and I was sure I'd find my way back easily.

Except, I didn't.

The streets all started to look the same, and my sense of direction betrayed me. I asked for help, but my broken Tibetan wasn't much use. The locals, kind as they were, gestured in different directions, leaving me even more confused. I wandered for what felt like hours, frustration creeping in.

Then, just as I was ready to resign myself to fate, an elderly monk appeared. Without saying a word, he motioned for me to follow him.

We walked in silence, weaving through the labyrinth of streets until, finally, the familiar sight of my guesthouse came into view.

I turned to thank him, but before I could speak, he simply smiled, pressed his hands together in a gesture of peace, and walked away.

That moment stayed with me—not just for the relief of finding my way, but for what it represented. **Sometimes, when you're lost, the best thing you can do is trust the kindness of strangers.**

The Kindness of Strangers in Turkey

If there's one thing travel has taught me, it's that people are inherently good. Yes, the world has its share of darkness, but more often than not, you find kindness in the most unexpected places.

One of the most heartwarming examples of this happened in **Istanbul, Turkey**. I had been wandering the Grand Bazaar, marveling at the explosion of colors and sounds—golden lanterns swaying from ceilings, the scent of rich spices, merchants calling out their best deals.

I must have looked particularly lost because an elderly shopkeeper suddenly approached me. With a warm smile, he gestured toward a small wooden stool beside his stall. "You look tired," he said in broken English. "Sit. Have tea."

I hesitated—after all, I didn't want to seem rude—but he insisted. Moments later, a steaming glass of **Turkish çay** was placed in my hands. We sat there, the old man speaking in a mix of Turkish and gestures, telling stories I could only half understand, but fully appreciate.

When I finally stood to leave, I reached for my wallet, but he shook his head. "No money," he said, smiling. "Guests are a gift."

That single act of generosity, of welcoming a stranger with nothing expected in return, reminded me why I travel—not just to see new places, but to experience the humanity that connects us all.

The Hardest Goodbye: Philadelphia's Streets

Of all my travels, one of the most difficult yet meaningful experiences was working with **Philadelphia's homeless**. The stories I heard, and the people I met, changed the way I saw the world.

When I first arrived in Philadelphia, I got lost almost immediately—straight from the airport. It was 10 PM, and I ended up wandering into a pretty rough part of the city. I must've looked completely out of place. A police car pulled up, and the officers didn't mince words: "You need to get out of this area. It's dangerous."

Just then, a black couple named Terena and Theo stepped in. They'd seen the commotion and offered to drive me to my accommodation, which was across the city. Over the next few days, they went even further—they showed me around Philly, brought me to their church, and even asked if I'd help feed the homeless.

I did. And it was one of the most humbling experiences of my life. Terena and Theo didn't know me, but they helped anyway. They saw a vulnerable stranger and responded with compassion. That kind of kindness? You don't forget it.

A Life of Stories, A Life Well Lived

Looking back at all these moments—the awe of standing before a silverback gorilla, the frustration of being lost in Tibet, the laughter of a shopkeeper in Turkey, Not the money. Not the status. Not even the destinations themselves.

But the stories.

The connections.

The moments that remind us that we are all human.

I have wandered through cities where history lingers in the air, sailed across oceans that stretch beyond the horizon and walked through villages where time moves at a different pace. And through it all, I've learned one undeniable truth:

The world is vast, beautiful, and full of kindness. And no matter how far I travel, that is the lesson I will carry with me always.

CHAPTER 11

LOOKING FORWARD

Life is a journey without a set destination. We spend our days moving forward, sometimes with purpose, sometimes simply following the road as it unfolds before us. And if I've learned anything from the experiences I've had, it's that the best adventures often happen when we least expect them.

Even now, after everything I've seen and done, I know there is still more waiting for me. More places to explore, more stories to collect, more moments to cherish. The past has shaped me, but the future is still mine to write.

Thoughts on Future Adventures

The thrill of exploration has never left me. My feet still itch to wander, my heart still longs for the unknown. There are places I have yet to visit, cultures I have yet to experience, and people I have yet to meet.

Bbut more than that, I want to keep **connecting with people**. Some of the most profound experiences I've had weren't just about where I was—they were about **who I was with**. Whether it was sharing tea with a shopkeeper in Turkey, or exchanging smiles with a gorilla in Uganda, those moments reminded me that life's greatest treasures are the relationships we build along the way.

I don't know where the road will lead next, but I know one thing: **I'll keep saying yes to the adventure**.

Final Reflections: Lessons from a Lifetime of Experiences

Looking back on my life, there are a few things I've come to understand—truths that have become my guiding principles.

1. **Resilience is everything:** Life will knock you down. It will take things from you that you never thought you could live without. But you get back up. You keep moving. And in the process, you find a strength you never knew you had.

59

2. **Kindness costs nothing but means everything.:** Some of the most powerful moments in my life have been the simplest—a warm smile, a helping hand, a conversation with a stranger. Small acts of kindness can change someone's entire world.
3. **Don't let one chapter define your whole story.:** For years, I carried the identity of the Milky Bar Kid like a badge. But I've learned that we are more than just one moment, one success, or one failure. We are the sum of everything we've lived, and our stories are always evolving.
4. **Never stop exploring.:** Whether it's traveling to a new country, learning a new skill, or stepping outside of your comfort zone, life is meant to be experienced. There is always something new to discover, both in the world and within yourself.
5. **Love fiercely, and don't be afraid to show it.:** I've lost people I loved dearly. I've learned the hard way that time is never guaranteed. So tell people how much they mean to you. Hold them close. Make the most of every moment.

The Road Ahead

I don't know what the future holds, but I do know this: **I will keep living, loving, and embracing every experience that comes my way.**

Because life isn't about standing still—it's about moving forward.

And I, for one, am excited to see where the journey takes me next.

Embracing the Unknown

As I stand on the threshold of the next chapter of my life, I find myself reflecting not just on where I've been, but on where I'm going. The world is still out there, vast and waiting, and though I may not move as fast as I once did, my heart still beats with the same sense of curiosity and wonder that it always has.

There is something beautiful about not knowing exactly what comes next. It means that every sunrise holds a new possibility, every encounter could lead to an unexpected adventure, and every step forward is another story waiting to be told.

I used to think that as I got older, I would settle, that I would lose the hunger to explore. But the truth is, the more I've seen, the more I've realized how much there still is to discover. The world is ever-changing, and so am I.

A Legacy Beyond Myself

If there's one thing I hope for in the years ahead, it's that the stories I've shared—through my travels, my experiences, and my life—will inspire others to live fully.

I want my children and grandchildren to know that life is not about waiting for things to happen, but about going out and making them happen. I want them to take risks, embrace both the joys and challenges of life, to never let fear keep them from pursuing their dreams.

I've always believed that our legacy isn't just in what we do, but in how we make people feel. I hope that when people think of me, they remember someone who lived passionately, who laughed loudly, who cared deeply, and who never stopped seeking adventure.

The Beauty of the Journey

If I've learned anything from my time on this earth, it's that **life is not measured by the milestones, but by the moments in between**.

It's in the quiet evenings spent reminiscing with loved ones. It's the conversations with strangers that turn into lifelong friendships. It's in the unexpected detours, the laughter-filled mishaps, and the small acts of kindness that leave lasting impressions.

I may never know exactly where the road will take me next, but I do know this—I will walk it with open arms, an open heart, and a readiness to embrace whatever comes my way.

Because in the end, it's not about reaching a destination.

It's about **enjoying the journey**.

PART – V

REFLECTIONS AND FUTURE

CHAPTER 12

REUNION AND REFLECTIONS

Time has a funny way of bringing things full circle. Decades had passed since my days as the Milky Bar Kid, yet that chapter of my life had never truly closed. It had followed me, shaped me, and, in many ways, defined me. But nothing could have prepared me for what it would feel like to step back into that world once more—to reunite with others who had worn the same cowboy hat and carried the same legacy.

The Milky Bar Kids Reunion: A Walk Through Time

The idea of a **Milky Bar Kids Reunion** had been floating around for some time, a nostalgic gathering of those who had played the iconic role over the years. It was an event designed to celebrate not just the history of the brand, but the stories of the kids who had once been part of it. And as I arrived at the venue, I felt a mix of excitement and apprehension.

What would it be like to see others who had lived a version of my childhood? Would they feel the same way about it as I did? Had their lives been shaped by those experiences as much as mine had?

Stepping into the room, I was met with a flood of memories. There they were—men of different ages, each with their own story, yet all bound by a single role that had, in one way or another, left an imprint on their lives. Some had gone on to pursue careers in acting, while others had taken entirely different paths. But for that night, we weren't actors or businessmen or fathers—we were the Milky Bar Kids, sharing a moment in time that had never truly left us.

We swapped stories, laughed at the absurdity of how a single childhood role had stayed with us for so long, and marveled at the old advertisements playing on a large screen in the background. Seeing my younger self, dressed in that cowboy outfit, delivering those famous lines—it was surreal.

But beyond the nostalgia, there was something deeper. It was a realization that, no matter where life had taken us, we all shared a unique experience—one that had shaped us, for better or worse, into the men we had become.

Reflections on Fame and Identity

As the night wore on, I found myself reflecting on the impact of that time in my life.

What had it really meant to be the Milky Bar Kid?

For some, it had been a fleeting moment of childhood fun, a role they left behind as they grew older. But for me, it had become a part of my identity. Being "Milky" wasn't just something I had done—it was something I had carried with me through every stage of life.

Fame, even at that level, has a way of leaving its mark. When you're known for something from such a young age, it shapes the way people see you—and, in turn, the way you see yourself.

There were times when I wondered what my life might have been like without it. Would I have taken a different path? Would I have built a different identity, separate from the one the world had given me?

But standing in that room, surrounded by others who had walked a similar path, I realized something important: **identity isn't just about the things we've done—it's about what we choose to carry forward**.

Being the Milky Bar Kid was part of my story, but it wasn't the whole story. And as much as I loved the nickname, the nostalgia, and the memories, I knew that the real legacy wasn't just in the ads or the recognition—it was in the way those experiences had shaped me into the person I had become.

The reunion wasn't just about looking back—it was about understanding how the past had led me to the present. And as I left that night, I felt a sense of peace. The Milky Bar Kid would always be a part of me, but **it was only one chapter in a much larger story**—a story still being written.

A Legacy Beyond the Screen

As I left the reunion that night, I couldn't help but replay the conversations in my mind. We had all walked different paths, yet there was a shared understanding between us—an unspoken connection built on nostalgia, fame, and the weight of being recognized for something we did as children.

Some of the other Milky Bar Kids had completely moved on, treating it as a fond but distant memory. Others, like me, had carried it as part of their identity, whether consciously or not. But what struck me the most was how, despite our differences, we all acknowledged the unique gift and burden that came with being part of something so iconic.

Fame, even in its smallest doses, leaves a lasting imprint. As a child, I never quite understood the significance of being the face of an entire brand. I was just a boy in a cowboy outfit, reciting lines and doing what I was told. But over the years, I began to realize that for many people, the Milky Bar Kid wasn't just a commercial—it was a memory from their own childhood.

I had been part of something bigger than myself. And perhaps that was why, even after all these years, the nickname still felt like home.

Balancing the Past with the Present

Leaving the reunion, I felt an overwhelming sense of gratitude—not just for the experience of being the Milky Bar Kid, but for the journey that had followed.

There had been struggles along the way. Losing Raine. The hardships of raising a family. The moments of loneliness and grief. The challenges of figuring out who I was beyond the image the world had given me. But through it all, I had **lived**—fully, deeply, and with an openness to experience that had shaped my entire life.

That night, I sat down with a drink in hand and thought about the younger version of myself—the little boy who had stood on that set, unaware of what was to come. What would he think of the man he had become?

I'd like to think he'd be proud.

Proud of the adventures. Proud of the resilience. Proud of the fact that, despite everything, I never let one chapter define the entire book.

Yes, I was Milky. But I was also a traveler, a father, a friend, a storyteller. And if there was one thing I had learned, it was that our identities are not fixed—they are ever-changing, shaped by the choices we make and the experiences we embrace.

Future Aspirations

I don't have any rigid plans for the future. Not because I'm lost or uncertain, but because I've been teaching myself to be more present—to truly sit with the moment, rather than be tugged backward by regret or pulled forward by worry. There's a quiet freedom in that, in simply existing here and now.

But still, the mind wanders. It's part of who I am—always wondering what's next, what horizon still waits for me, what unknown street I might one day walk down with wide eyes and a racing heart. I find myself daydreaming about the next adventure, sketching out mental maps of places I haven't yet touched, flavors I haven't tasted, and moments I haven't yet lived.

There are places that call out to me, softly but persistently.

Japan, once more. I've been before, but it feels incomplete. I want to see the country blushing in cherry blossoms and walk beneath those pale pink clouds as petals fall like whispers to the ground. I imagine myself sitting beneath a tree in Tokyo, sipping matcha, watching the delicate chaos of petals swirling in the breeze—a fleeting beauty that demands you stop and appreciate the present.

Bhutan, the mountain kingdom. There's a stillness there I long to feel—a quiet wisdom tucked between snow-capped peaks and fluttering prayer flags. I picture myself trekking up steep paths, breathless not just from the altitude but from the staggering beauty all around. I want to sit in a monastery high above the clouds and listen to the silence, to the whispers of wind and wisdom carried through the valleys.

Nigeria calls me, too—perhaps more personally. It's part of my girlfriend's heritage, a place alive with energy, color, music, and depth.

I want to experience it not as a passing tourist but with roots and connection, to see the country through her eyes, to understand the culture and stories that helped shape her.

And then there's North Korea. A strange dream, maybe, but curiosity doesn't care for borders. If and when it becomes accessible, I want to go—not out of spectacle-seeking, but out of genuine curiosity. I want to see what life is like beyond the headlines, beyond the narrative we're fed. I want to meet the people, hear their stories, and see, even there, the shared humanity we all carry.

Of course, beyond these, the world remains wide open. Maybe I'll find myself somewhere I never planned. Maybe the most memorable journeys are the ones that weren't penciled into itineraries but stumbled into by chance. That's the beauty of it—the not knowing.

So no, I have no fixed map for the future. Just an open heart, a curious mind, and a suitcase that's always half-packed, waiting for the next call of the road.

The Power of Storytelling

As I reflected on my life and future aspirations, I realized that everything I had done—the travels, the encounters, the moments of struggle and triumph—had given me something invaluable: **stories**.

Stories that connected me to people, that made others laugh, cry, or feel a sense of kinship. Stories that reminded me of the incredible journey I had taken. And stories that, hopefully, would continue to inspire those who heard them.

That's what life is, after all—a collection of stories, some sweet, some bitter, but all meaningful in their way.

And as I sat there, thinking about everything that had led me to this moment, I smiled. Because no matter what came next, one thing was certain: **the story wasn't over yet.**

EPILOGUE

A Life Well Lived

As I look back on my journey—the highs and lows, the triumphs and losses, the adventures and quiet moments—I see a life that has been anything but ordinary. I have been many things: a child star, a traveler, a father, a friend. But more than anything, I have been a seeker—of experiences, of connection, of meaning.

If there is one lesson I want to leave behind, it is this: **Live fully. Take the risk. Say yes to the adventure. Love without hesitation. And never stop exploring—both the world and yourself.**

Every challenge I faced taught me resilience. Every place I visited expanded my understanding of life. Every person I met left an imprint on my soul. And through it all, I have come to realize that life isn't about waiting for things to happen—it's about creating your own story, one moment at a time.

A Message to Readers

To those who have followed my journey through these pages, I want to say thank you. Thank you for allowing me to share my story, for walking with me through my memories, and for taking the time to see the world through my eyes.

If there is anything you take away from this book, let it be this: **Life is unpredictable, but that is what makes it beautiful. Embrace it. Chase your dreams. Love deeply. And always, always keep moving forward.**

No matter where you are in your own journey, know that you are never alone. The world is full of stories, and yours is still being written.

Now go out there—and make it a good one.

APPENDICES

Photographs and Memorabilia

(Insert spaces for pictures from significant life events, travels, and personal milestones.)

- **Childhood & Milky Bar Kid Days:** *(Include early childhood photos, behind-the-scenes images from the Milky Bar Kid era, and reunion pictures.)*

- **Family & Personal Life:** *(Photos of my daughters, family gatherings, and meaningful personal moments.)*

- **Travels & Adventures:** *(Images from Colombia, Moscow, Tibet, Uganda, and other journeys around the world.)*

- **Volunteer Work & Reflections:** *(Snapshots from my time helping the homeless in Philadelphia, along with other acts of service.)*

DOWN THE
MEMORY LANE

Alaska – 1999

Antarctica – 2003

Cambodia Ankor Wart – 2002

Cappadocia – 2023

Iceland – 2000

New Zealand – 2000

Petra, Jordan – 2000

Pyramids of Giza, Egypt – 2000

Mongolia – 2009

Great Wall of China – 2001

Swiss Alps Matterhorn - 2023

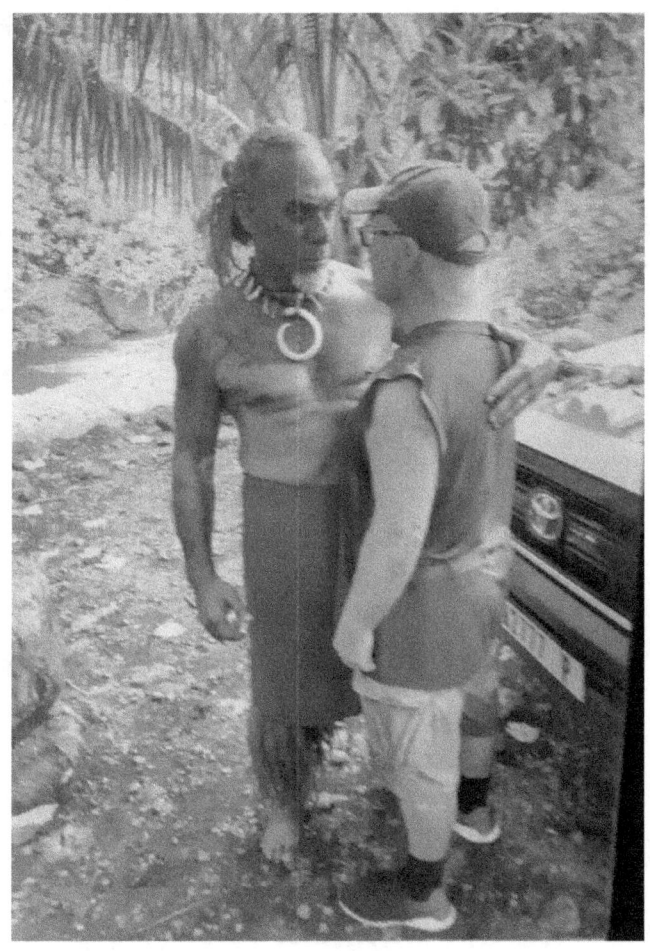

Tahiti – 2024

The Everglades, Florida – 2024

Sahara Desert – 2004

Taj Mahal, India – 2006

Me as A Kid – 1964

Me (top left), at the Kids' Reunion – 1986

Me in Las Vegas, USA, as A Much Older "Kid" – 2003

My Mum and Dad on Their Wedding Day – 1952

My Daughters: Brooke (left) and Raine (right) – 1986

My Raine – 1986

Me and My Raine in Tenerife – 1986

Me (bottom left), When I Had Hair – 1974

My Brooke on Her Wedding Day – 2023

My Grandson, Dexter. Aged 4 – 2024

Dexter – 2024

Me Finishing the London Marathon – 1990

Me, Hayley (my first wife), and My Two Girls, Tenerife – 1985

Me, Violy (my second wife), and Her Kids. Our Marriage Day,
Philippines – 2004

Addy, My Current Girlfriend, Miami – 2024

ART GALLERY

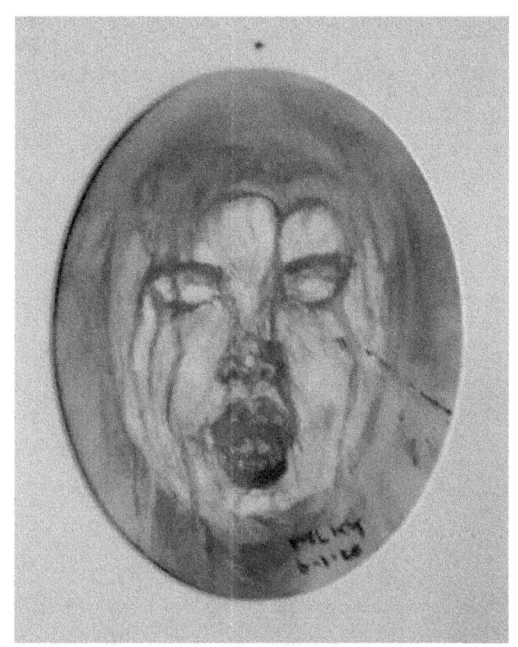

www.ingramcontent.com/pod-product-compliance
Lightning Source LLC
Chambersburg PA
CBHW072011170626
46813CB00005B/2113